I have been an avid reader all of my life, but somewhere along the line I was inspired to pick up the pen for myself. I drew upon the familiar. Having been raised as a young child in South America, my familiarity with the Americas was already there: my love of Westerns and the lives of that genre provided a comfort blanket, inspiring me to write this book.

I love family dynamics. As a youngster, I watched my parents and relatives in awe as they baked, cooked, made clothes, nurtured plants, drove cars, maintained the home, braided hair into beautiful cornrows and one-you styles. All these gentle gifts are a 'Thank You' for all their efforts in creating a lovely world for me.

This book is dedicated to both of my parents.

Christina Hicks

RED LETTER DAY

AUSTIN MACAULEY PUBLISHERS
LONDON * CAMBRIDGE * NEW YORK * SHARJAH

Copyright © Christina Hicks 2025

The right of Christina Hicks to be identified as author of this work has been asserted by the author in accordance with sections 77 and 78 of the Copyright, Designs and Patents Act 1988.

All rights reserved. No part of this publication may be reproduced, stored in a retrieval system, or transmitted in any form or by any means, electronic, mechanical, photocopying, recording, or otherwise, without the prior permission of the publishers.

Any person who commits any unauthorised act in relation to this publication may be liable to criminal prosecution and civil claims for damages.

This is a work of fiction. Names, characters, businesses, places, events, locales, and incidents are either the products of the author's imagination or used in a fictitious manner. Any resemblance to actual persons, living or dead, or actual events is purely coincidental.

A CIP catalogue record for this title is available from the British Library.

ISBN 9781035890552 (Paperback)
ISBN 9781035890569 (ePub e-book)

www.austinmacauley.com

First Published 2025
Austin Macauley Publishers Ltd®
1 Canada Square
Canary Wharf
London
E14 5AA

'Red Letter Day' means a day that is noteworthy. It contains five heart-warming stories that capture a genre of America from the mid-19th century onwards, when many lives were lived 'on a wing and a prayer.'

This book may contain outdated cultural depictions that reflect attitudes at the time.

Table of Contents

Dilly's Secret 11

The Signature Cowboy Hat 16

Old Grandma Cesserley 23

The Cowboy Showman 30

That's My Man 40

My Hero 61

Dilly's Secret

Her father Wingate had sat her down that morning; he began explaining that during her mother's illness he had prayed fervently that her suffering would diminish, that she would make a full recovery. But after the doctor diagnosed untreatable spinal meningitis, it seemed he would have to accept this hand that he'd been dealt and somehow carry on without her.

But it was near impossible for a grown man to do house chores, keep the stock, gather kindling, keep a ranch and look after a young child – he needed help and that would eventually come in the shape of Cara. This former bookkeeper from Baltimore had experienced this lifestyle prior to finding her calling in business.

"Now please don't be put off by her funny ways—she just likes to improve things as she goes along. Did you not notice how I have me a starched, ironed shirt on and a bolo tie buckle? I'm not some yokel anymore, not now she's in my life. No, sir."

"Cara has been staying in town at the Makenzie Hotel with all her belongings hauled up at the livery under lock and key. We had a quiet union and now she's just itching to get out here to meet you." He reflected on what had been said and attempted to smooth it over by adding, "You're not always going to be ten; you need a grown woman in the house to show you womanly things to add to what your mother taught you."

"I know you can sew a good chambray dress, shirts, darn and make beautiful doilies from your needlepoint—which I have had framed all around the house—but Cara is very fancy—get yourself ready for a complete overhaul!"

At noon, a whole troop of carriages carrying her belongings preceded by a black buggy with leather rustles along the sides, a shining ornate mahogany wood carriage and her beaming face topped by a magnificent church hat with ostrich feathers arrived.

The question Dilly thought—what did she not bring? She had never seen such a spectacle and was not used to it. She had never even ventured into town, only being allowed last birthday to go with her father out to the old trading post in their humble bare wagon.

Four regal black draft horses with black leather and copper hitching bowed as she, Ms Cara, accepted Wingate's hand to dismount.

"Use your imagination, Dilly," her new mother, Ms Cara, sang as she swept through the house, her eyes appraising all she saw before her. "That's all it will take to make a real home. I will work my magic from room to room; I will introduce floral wallpaper, put rugs on the floor and have a velvet seating area as part of the extension we plan to undertake. This house is going to be wonderful."

"But first things first, my little girl. You're coming to town with me to get all the things we need to, how shall we say, soften those rough edges of yours." Ms Cara came by and waved her lacy fan in Dilly's direction by her comely face.

Mother—Ms Cara—had talked up the visit to town—how they would enjoy weekly visits to the mercantile store, how it had everything and anything needed could be sourced there. That Dilly's dowdy jean clothing, which granted, had been made lovingly under the instruction of her mother, needed a revamp! No more kelots or chambray dresses for her. They would secure a decent wardrobe of clothes and a good Sunday dress because, as of now, they, the whole family, will be attending church.

………

Dilly would steal away most mornings past the coral down to the rocky stream, a place she and her younger brother used to play each day, doing belly flops and practicing their diving skills like water babies before he died from an ear infection caused by La Grippe… now Dilly frequented the stream alone out of rebelliousness to Ms Cara, as she refused to be seated in the huge shiny roll-top tin bath her stepmother had brought with her from Baltimore. She called it 'refreshment' throwing out the old for the new, pooh-poohing the traditional jug and bowl for that modern contraption.

She had taken a large tin cup of her urine from the overnight slop bucket and poured the contents over her wet bowed head as she crocheted at the stream, massaging it in. Then she swam a doggy paddle a few lengths. Her mother had shown her how to live off the land and create beautiful, shiny, conditioned gold locks. "Better than any beauty parlour…" her mother claimed. It was their secret.

That night before the big day Dilly wound up brown parcel paper and curled her sectioned hair around the strips tightly, finishing with a large knot, held together snugly under her white sleeping cap.

There was tangible excitement in the air the morning of the trip. Ms Cara was giddy as a school girl with a beaming smile on her face. It took a full two hours starting with her bath, then the lotions, the corset, the hair, the makeup application and then the dressing, to the final 'spritz' of perfume. Then she appeared out of her bedroom with a contented smile.

....

They boarded the black carriage, which her father had hitched himself and they set off without any further ado. The Mercantile Store stood on one level, very large, right in the middle of town.

As you entered the foyer of the Mercantile Store, a bell chimed. Dilly was enveloped by the wonderful aroma of sandalwood coming off the Perfumery Counter. There were long displays of phonographs on one side and beautiful ornate carpet bags on the other.

The lady of the store, Mrs. Gillespie, waved both hands in the air. "Good day, Cara!" Immediately, she recognised her, as she was also a fellow lady of good breeding. She beckoned them over through the haberdashery, fabrics, to the bonnets and hats. In passing, Dilly had never seen such a huge selection of bolts of fabric: burlap, khaki, calico, muslin, gaberdine, satin, silk, gingham and Chantilly laces.

"Just as we discussed—a Sunday bonnet for this young lady to start, please," Ms Cara announced. On cue, Dilly removed her flimsy beret and hid it by her side. "My, I do declare," squealed Mrs Gillespie in a shrill audible tone. "…you have the most B-e-a-u-t-i-f-u-l HAIR!" Dilly had a flashback of herself pouring a tin of urine onto her wet locks at the stream and her eyes darted to one side to Ms Cara, then to the other at Mrs Gillespie, who was caressing one long ringlet in the palm of her hand. Dilly's cheek flushed bright red.

The Signature Cowboy Hat

Norland and his wife Kayla were God-fearing people who made a great effort to attend church each Sunday. The test came in the fall and then winter when traveling conditions were at their worst. They had proved over time that they were not just 'fair weather parishioners.' Their reward after years of committed attendance: the Reverend offered jobs to them within the church. Kayla taught Sunday school and Norland was made an usher.

Another of the church attendees, Jet, the local mercantile owner, extended a hand to receive a parcel from Kearth, the village postmaster. "Thanking you kindly," he said, pulling at the cord, folding away the brown parcel paper to reveal a large catalogue sent all the way from Chicago. It was splendid, with large stipple and crosshatch illustrations of numerous garments and underclothes printed in black ink onto white blotting paper. As the weeks wore on, Jet raved about the new catalogue and insisted the customers, whether yellow, black, or white, take time to behold this thing of beauty.

Jet had been in 'sales' nearly all his life in one shape or another and had travelled around the 'Circuit Algorithm' up and down the country of the US as a traveling salesman, selling bricks out of a suitcase, a job requiring dogged commitment and resilience. He had the gift of the gab for sure. Finally, after many years on the road, he severed all ties with the brick company but not before he himself bought enough bricks to build this mercantile store up from the ground. It was his pride and joy.

The store layout was key and he had insisted on not just one entrance but two.

The second entrance was placed at the side of the building closest to a school run route, a thoroughfare that all the local children would encounter in the morning and in the afternoon while making their way into town.

There were double glass doors on that side with ornate wrought iron handles and windows painted with the choice of drinks: soda, draft sarsaparilla and lemonade. The mahogany floors were stained a dark brown and kept immaculate. Alongside one wall were velveteen-padded high stools.

There were jars and jars containing stick candy, sherbet lemons, liquorice comfits, black jacks, cola cubes, wine gums and gobstoppers. Thick glass domes sat on the glass countertop with homemade peach cobbler, apple pie and ringed doughnuts. It was truly a feast for the eyes and the children flocked and stood in an orderly line waiting to recite the order they had dreamt of all day while at school, with mouths agape. Jet took great pride in making the children's dreams come true and being their source of happiness.

Norland and Kayla both enjoyed getting 'gussied up' for the great outing of the week—to attend church. Kayla owned two hat boxes containing hats that had matching dresses in her wardrobe. "You should invest in a hat box, Norland," Kayla protested, rocking on her chair doing needlepoint. "The wedding of Beth MacKensey is coming next month and you're going to need a nice place to put your new hat when you get it. You won't be able to leave this one lying around waiting to be sat on," she chided. "We have a bigger budget this time around due to the rise last month going through."

"It can't be too dark, as I want to pair it with my grey suit," Norland noted. "I'll drop by the mercantile store and see what hat I can find to match it in the morning."

The next morning before Norland went to work, he went into the mercantile store and waited by the counter. Jet soon appeared through the bamboo divider from out back. "Norland, wait until I introduce you to the first and very interesting apparel catalogue I have been sent all the way from Chicago."

"I need a hat," Norland said.

"What kind of hat will you be investing in today?"

"A grey formal hat – I already have a couple of leather ones and this bowland," he said. "I need something light grey."

Jet opened the catalogue. "Do you see what I see?" he exclaimed before letting out a chuckle as he turned the book upside down. "Hat number three," he said, pointing to an illustration of a grey Silverbelly Cowboy hat. Norland bent low to read the small print: "This hat is sure to add a touch of vibrant Western style to any outfit."

"The craftsmanship," Jet said. "See that beautiful suede? And the silver buckles on that Mexican ribbon detail?" he inquired again.

"I see it…" said Norland.

"It is a hat of real distinction – to be worn where?" Jet inquired, turning the catalogue back around.

"To church – of course – a wedding."

"Then you'll have the sharpest and best headdress of any man there," Jet said, playing it up. "Now you know I would need to put in an order? It could take as long as two weeks, so it's good you came in today. Small, medium, or large?"

"OK, I'm sold on it – medium, put my order through," Norland said, reaching into his jacket pocket to bring out his money bag.

"Will there be anything else? A suit perhaps? It will only take a few minutes for me to organise the fitting."

"I already have a good suit. That should cover it."

"Thanking you kindly," Jet said, snapping the catalogue shut and depositing the money in the till. As Norland turned to leave, Willard from the lumber mill was making his way to the counter. "Howdy," Norland said, touching the brim of his boland. Willard said good morning to Jet and proceeded to place his order.

"I need a new hat," Norland heard him say just before the bell above the entrance door drowned out the rest of the conversation; he shut the door behind him.

Norland went straight to his printing office, which he set up four years ago, having cut loose from an overpopulated boom town in search of more genteel clientele, as it seemed the majority of his day was spent liaising with the Marshall and printing 'Wanted' posters. Here, the hired help was Mathias, who dealt with the printing blocks and occasionally his wife, Justina, would help out with the proofreading. Norland had developed his skill set and now offered a book-binding service in addition to the writing of the Weekly Chronicle. Though his bread-and-butter regular commissions came from clergy all over the county wanting Bibles printed and bound.

He hung up his jacket and pulled on two dark cloth shirt protectors over his arms and began picking up where he left off typesetting the day before.

....

The morning of the wedding, Norland and his wife dressed carefully. He helped her by closing the clasp of her necklace and she handed him the box containing his new hat. "And such a lovely box for them to send your new hat in," Kayla commented. Norland slicked down his handlebar moustache and placed the hat on his head, displaying his cocktail cuffs on his tailored shirt. Kayla smoothed down the winged shirt collars underneath his grey jacket with a look of admiration. "I think we're there," he said, glancing at his gold pocket watch. "Shall we?" he said while placing his wife's grey Pelese cloak over her shoulders. He offered her his arm and they made their way through the parlour.

......

Four well-dressed Church Sisters milled around the empty Church – the blinds had not been pulled yet, so it set an intimate glow along the Pulpit. The Church was the central hub of the community: births, deaths and everything in between; marriage, also Sunday school, town meetings and prayer meetings. The parishioners flocked there like geese for prayer, solace and divine guidance as the Reverend delivered his sermon faithfully Sunday after Sunday.

But there was nothing more exhilarating than when the seasons changed and the Church Revival time rolled around.

Families sat in the heat, transfixed to the rostrum as individuals took to the stage to give rousing testimonies on how their lives had been transformed by the grace of God. Mothers fanned themselves wildly, children fell asleep across their laps. As the visiting circuit Preachers held Bibles aloft whilst sermonising, the menfolk patted their wet brows with white handkerchiefs. The organist, who had been loaned out to them especially and had come from some distance to help, played melodic tunes fast then slow to help the expounding Preacher and to play well-known Church hymns that got the congregation clapping.

A group of children rushed in with freshly picked flowers the Sisters had instructed them to find, to add last minute to wedding arch foliage. White and yellow satin bows were displayed on the side of each pew to match and there were vases of flowers resting on two wooden sideboard cabinets. When the ladies had done all that was needed they sat themselves down to wait for their husbands to join them for the greatly anticipated wedding march.

A morning service, long before high noon meant that everything and everyone was cool and fresh and eager for the proceeding wedding to take place before the sun had a chance to sap the life out of the day. Each Church Pew had a number of Bibles and Hymn books placed there. Those already there spoke politely under their breath and Norland tipped his hat to Jet who sat further up the front of the Church with his wife.

As they were not relatives, Norland and Kayla hung back and opted to sit a respectful distance away at the back of the Church, arm in arm. Kayla admired the beautiful wedding arch which stood in place of the Altar. Then it struck her, "Isn't that Horace the Druggist with the exact same hat on his head as yours?" she whispered under her breath. "…and there, Silas the Bookkeeper has your hat on his head!" she exclaimed, pulling at Norland's arm. Norland looked up to where she nodded. He spotted Willard the Lumberjack in the same hat too. Then Mankins the Shoemaker walked in with his wife, his head adorned with the 'said' hat! Suddenly it seemed that nearly all the men seated in the Church had on Norland's grey Silverbelly Cowboy hat with matching grey suits!

Kayla gripped Norland's arm whilst she craned her neck—eyes like saucers, her mouth agape, staring. "I thought you bought the hat from out of town?" she protested, whispering into his ear.

"I thought I had. Looks like all us men have the same taste in hats!"

The church piano began playing and drowned out his exclamation, the bride holding a posy in one hand and her father with the other walked in slowly. Norland thought to himself, I can't say us men lacked imagination—it's just 'pot luck' all of us arriving like it was a fancy dress—everyone turning up in the same outfit!

"I knew living in a small, hick town had its downsides," Norland said, rolling his eyes.

Old Grandma Cesserley

Cesserley sat on a long bench on the porch, she kept turning the handle of the wooden butter churn. Her eyes were drawn to the white clouds in the sky, they looked like white cotton candy against the bluest backdrop.

Opposite her was the last of her granddaughters—the baby of the family—Grace. She sat on the wooden beams of the raised porch, both legs dangling, shelling peas into a bowl.

"Your grandfather and I were some of the earliest prospectors there in Kansas. We set out there together two days after our wedding – well, I say wedding. There was much revelry on both sides of the family. We did it like the collared folks did – cheap and cheerful." She hitched her long dress up higher over her knees. "We just jumped over a broom." She let out a cackle. The granddaughter looked up and giggled. "Horrice packed up a set of tools donated to him from his kin – shovel, pickaxe, dynamite, wheelbarrow, tin pan, even an old shotgun! We collected wood along the way. I was his 'helpmate', just as it says in the good book. As I organised the rations and got to cooking, Horrice would throw down a tune or two on his mouth organ; the fancy name is harmonica. We slept in the wagon each night after a day of prospecting. I sure loved those nights; after supper, we would look up to the sky at the stars and just talk – it was a lovely way to pass the time. Of course, each month the outfit grew and grew; we had to rip up all the rules and begin to look out just for ourselves. But there was great intrigue each day when Horrice would open up that leather pouch to show me the day's takings. Soon we had to bury those nuggets under the wagon in a wooden box…" She paused. "See that bucket of water? Peel those yellow potatoes for me and drop them in there." She patted her brow with the back of her hand. "Turn came when folks just walked in on us with barley coats on their backs – let alone slickers or galoshes boots. Gold fever had come upon us and they all rushed in with a whole lot of enthusiasm and very little equipment. Thick as plates – the lot of them. That night Horrice held me in his arms before bedtime and he looked at me. Then he rested his forehead against mine. We both knew what we had to do. We pulled on our coats, dug up our booty, saddled the horses and hauled ass out of there as fast as we could." Cesserley paused and rested from the turning for a second. "All in all, six months of hard grafting had given us the equivalent of six years' wages, which we banked up pretty quick. We travelled to Nebraska Territory and bought a boarding house in the frontier town. Heard later that they called the place not too far from where we staked our claim - 'Dodge City' – it was said to be a hotbed of lawless activity. There was no law enforcement there, you see; even the military had no jurisdiction over the town. We were pleased we got away. In 1857, aged 22, I sired my first child – a boy, your first uncle – Dalphont, such a lovely baby – real comely; he died, though, of crib death - so sad. Then your Uncle Stanford appeared out of nowhere and, last, five years later, your mother Sukee. Horrice convinced me to let him go dig for gold again. "It ain't no flash in the pan; let me go whilst the stream is full. You've got to speculate to accumulate," he said with a big grin on his face. So he left me in the charge of one of his cousins and took off there. That was the last I saw of him. They say he died of cholera but I believe it was foul play."

"Oh Granny – Cess, I'm sorry," Grace said, dropping the last potato into the bucket of water. She placed a hand on her forehead to pull back a wisp of hair.

"Never did get his body back – such a shame. All I have to remember him by is the bone pipe he loved to smoke with. Sometime when I get a real hankering for him, I will go out to the back of the barn, look in that old suitcase, rummage around in his old sack jacket for that bone pipe he loved so much." Cesserley sighed and took a rest before she let the freshly made butter flop into an enamel dish. "I'd better get this in the pantry before it melts." As she lifted her old frame, a caller came into view. "Good day, ma'am. I have a telegraph for you."

"Oh my!" Cesserley exclaimed, "I wonder who it's from," she said, taking the brown envelope from the postmaster's young assistant. "Can I offer you a coolant?"

"Thank you kindly, a glass of what you're having will go down nicely," he said, looking at the bench where a jug sat in a tray with glasses. Cesserley lifted the muslin cover off the jug and poured lemonade out for him. The assistant stretched over the lily-of-the-valley shrub and took the glass and downed it straight away. Grace smiled, taking the empty glass from him. "Thank you."

"And thank you kindly," Cesserley replied, holding up the envelope. "Grace," she said, "oblige me, read out this telegraph for me. Let's make haste and get this butter put away…"

They both went through the flyscreen and into the house, which always seemed to remain cool even in the heat of the day. Grace trailed slowly behind as she opened the note. "It's from Uncle Stanford in Tulsa; he would like you to visit him to arrive in time for their daughter Morgana's Debutants Day…" Grace looked up at Cesserley, who had closed the door to the pantry. "After your Granddaddy died," she continued, "I thought it best to send your Uncle Stanford to a private school – the boy needed to be amongst respectable men. So, I sold up the boarding house to the railway company when they came a-knocking. I believe it was worth it, to have Stanford grow up disciplined and brave, showing the makings of gallantry…to be a well-educated gentleman. He got in through the 'backdoor'," she said in a conspiratorial tone. "I paid for all his education up front; they couldn't refuse me, he was a full boarder…it was just something I had to do, not only for Stanford but for the memory of his older brother, Dalphont. I migrated here with your mother. The last time I went out to him was for his graduation – he stepped out that day looking fine – and – dandy," Cesserley said with a proud grin on her lips. "I had better think about packing…help me, Grace!" she exclaimed, starting to get excited. "I need my newest and best apparel and that blessed corset. That thing always takes my breath away but I guess it would be worth it. Stanford kept himself to himself though – I've never met his wife, Murella, or his daughter Morganna. I'm very much looking forward to meeting them both in the flesh for the first time."

Cesserley knew it would be a grand affair as she boarded the carriage at the station. It was not long before she viewed Stanford's sprawling homestead. The introductions were formal; only Murella gave her a welcoming peck on both cheeks. Morganna curtseyed politely. Cesserley maintained a genuine smile as they exchanged pleasantries, then she climbed the sweeping steps, following the maid as she was shown to the guest room.

The Debutante Cotillion was to take place in one of the great halls at her granddaughter's college. The many tables were covered with white cotton tablecloths; the crockery, salt and pepper shakers were all set out in an orderly fashion. "Bone China," Cesserley commented as she sat at one of the many tables. Stanford sat himself down after sliding the seat neatly beneath his mother's bustles and then beneath his wife.

"What a lavish affair, Stanford," Cesserley said, eyeing the diamond stick pin on his formal attire. "All the well-heeled guests are here," he retorted.

"Do you have a bow yet, dear?" Cesserley enquired of Morganna.

"Father says I must prioritise my studies above matters of the heart."

"And rightly so," Stanford said, reaching out and grasping Murella's hand. "You're just getting started; why jeopardise your future by becoming a wife and mother when we have lavished all of this education on you?"

"There's plenty of time for that later," Murella added.

Cesserley nodded her head. Stanford produced a velvet box from his pocket and placed it before Morganna. "Your mother and I want this to be a day for you to remember, always." Morganna opened the small box, revealing a pair of pear-shaped diamond earrings. "I love this," she said, glancing up at both parents. She rose to leave for her line-up and hugged both of them before she slipped away.

"Mother, Murella, I have been elected to read tonight's speech," Stanford said as he rose from his seat, happy in the knowledge that the ladies would get on famously; they had a lot of catching up to do this evening. He strode off to the presentation stand, his suit tails flapping, past the lines of Baroque red Rococo upholstered chairs where the young debutantes sat in alphabetical order. He gave Morganna a wink as he reached into his breast pocket to produce a speech. He tapped a fluted glass with a knife and waited for the room to settle. "A warm welcome to each of you on this special Mother's Day weekend. What a wonderful and gorgeous day to start the Debutante Season. The girls here today will be selected not just for social standing but for their own achievements as well as special talents…integras – Integrity, showing honesty, excellence. Virtus – Virtue, showing goodness, morality. Grata," he proceeded, "Greatness, not measured by wealth but by character. The virtues that will carry you through every decision you make in your life…the alumni, some of the founders here today with your sons and daughters, this ball is a gathering of all equally minded families. One of the most prominent social events of the year. After we have sung the American anthem, it will be my pleasure to introduce them to you."

The evening wore on and Cesserley became very sentimental. If only Horace had been here to experience what she had just witnessed and heard, what a swarah! She dabbed a tear from her cheek with a satin-gloved hand. It was evident that she had made the right decision by Stanford—he had turned out to be everything she hoped and prayed for—but she could not help but feel a pang of guilt that she had been the one who survived to witness it. She rose from the chaise longue that she had been seated on, enjoying watching the dances of the young ones and made an exit through a glass patio door to take in the night air.

She did what seemed natural to her after experiencing such emotion, looking up at the black velvet sky, the many diamond-dotted stars that shone there. She reached into her drawstring pouch and produced Horrice's bone pipe – she thought she would commune with him in the only way he would appreciate now. So, feeding a little tobacco into the bowl, alighting it and pulling softly and lovingly on the mouthpiece, she glanced at the night sky. It was as if Horrice were there beside her himself. Now she was at peace.

"Mother! What is that? Pipe?" Stanford vocalised incredulously from behind her. Cesserley turned to him with a start.

"What are you smoking?" he said, with disbelief at his mother's vulgarity.

"It's tobacco of course – what do you think I was smoking, tumbleweed?"

Stanford's face softened then he smiled at the retort. "Would you believe this was your father's pipe?" Cesserley said, softening. Lacing her arm through Stanford's, she let the embers fall slowly onto the ground. "I'll tell you the story," she said, smiling too.

The Cowboy Showman

"Who goes there?" the Groundsman enquired, holding up his kerosene lantern. There was silence – the only response came from the crickets chirping in the cool night air. The Groundsman's lips tightened again over his cigar. Then he heard the cracking of a twig away by the trees; his sweaty, potted face opened up again and he repeated the call. "Who goes there?" Slowly, from behind a tree, a figure emerged – a woman in a green, bell-shaped tea skirt and a white mantilla wrap hanging over her head to protect her from the elements began moving towards him. She was clutching something. The Groundsman thought at first it was a pet; then, on closer inspection, he realised it was a new-born niño wrapped tightly in swaddling clothes. The woman raised her head, looking directly at him with sorrowful eyes; she moved her billowy shirt arm to place her finger beneath the baby's face. "I'm so sorry." She gasped. "Please give my baby to the Nuns, Señor," she said, pointing to the Nunnery in the distance with her chin. The Groundsman threw the cheroot cigar stub away from his lips in an instant and retorted, "What? You are not married?"

"I am very married, Señor. I cannot keep my husband off me; the only form of contraception I have are my nails," she said, swiping her hand downwards. "Please, this child is just another hungry mouth to feed," she appealed and began weeping. The Groundsman's heavy-set body moved forward and immediately reached out to clasp the baby. "Please forgive me," the woman said, covering her cheeks with both hands before darting off again into the night.

The Groundsman watched her disappear back into the shadows.

....

As he marched back to his home, his thoughts flooded through; all his secret desires that he had nursed over the years were being fulfilled, however—not in the order he had anticipated. He had gone through the phase of longing for a child for years with his wife and only in later life did they finally conceive. But the trauma of the birth snatched her and the child away from him due to complications. The nuns themselves at the nunnery had attended to her in the infirmary but the amount of blood loss was too great.

The groundsman had even taken the time to prepare a nursery for the impending birth and even after coming to terms with such a devastating loss of the two souls on the same night, he had left the room untouched—crib, soft toys and all. Now the Good Lord blessed him with another niño. As he walked into the house to the nursery, he took a seat in the rocking chair he had made for his wife Elva and allowed himself to chuckle; the chuckle soon turned into a belly laugh. The mysterious lady had left him plentiful joy and happiness in her wake! The baby stirred. "Come, my little one," he said, raising the baby up to the nape of his neck. "I will take care of you tonight," he cooed. But what was it? He was arrested by the sudden question. "What are you?" He was not sure. He rose and quickly set down the infant on the changing block. Gently, he unwound the swaddling and opened the knotted nappy as if he were inspecting a handkerchief full of gold nuggets—"a boy!" He sighed, straightening and a smile of acknowledgment crept across his lips.

....

Salvetor opened the large wooden Ottoman. Along the top were items of clothing, including a folded fringed buckskin cowboy outfit. Underneath all the clothing was an assortment of firearms. "I was never a gunslinger," he confided to Nino. "But I knew my way around a revolver and pistol. My father trained me well when I was young, like you."

"He would say, "Salvetor, you're cutting your teeth, even if you miss the target. It takes years of practice to get the skills—I will start training with you." Salvetor held up a leather bandolier. "This can be adjusted." He noted, sitting himself down beside the Ottoman closer to Nino; he propped his back up on the end of the bed. "Nino, you must learn how to hunt and how to defend yourself with a pistol. Learn to take it apart and clean every bit," he said, squinting down the gun's exposed barrel.

"That's the only way to expect the best results from it." He pointed the Colt and then snapped the barrel shut. Nino pulled a cowboy boot up towards him and pushed a spur with his finger so it reeled around for a second. "I have been plugged—once!" Salvetor declared, moving his billowy vaquero shirt nape to expose keloid skin left by the injury on his shoulder. "I was mistaken for a rustler. Never again did I go walking around after dark on other people's land. I said to myself I'm too young to leave this terra firma, all because a few horses were spooked."

Salvetor continued to instruct Nino. Then he rose to his feet. "Let's go out now and do some practicing." He pulled out the revolver with a box of cartridges and some for the Colt pistol too. "If you bring that basket in the kitchen by the stove, you will find some empty bean tins and empty tequila bottles I have been saving."

Outside, Salvator placed the tins along some boulders at the rear of the house and demonstrated his firing expertise at various distances away from the boulders. Nino watched, his eyes on stalks and his mouth agape. He gave his father a look of admiration while nodding and whispering, "Yes, Papa," to confirm he understood all that was being explained. Salvator, his surrogate father, displayed patience and composure while instructing the boy.

When finally Nino was allowed to handle the pistol, he inhaled deeply and squared his small frame, then his shoulders, to balance himself against the weight he had been entrusted with. Beads of perspiration appeared on his top lip as he listened intently to his father's instruction. This was his first parlay with a pistol; he exhaled, the recoil sent him flying. When he landed on his rear, he felt alive and elated. He knew then that firearms were something he had great respect for and something he wanted to master.

....

Nino stood at the side of the house some distance away, his head bowed low as a mark of respect. For he stood on Holy

Ground; his father had breathed his last breath in the house peacefully where he had been raised. Nino heard him say the words, "I'm going for it…" The nuns had helped organise a well-turned-out funeral and the despertar—wake was to be later in the afternoon.

Nino looked at his mother Elva's grave beside his father's freshly dug one. He knew he was looking at this scene for the last time but prayed, as a mark of respect, that the scene would remain with him in his mind's eye wherever he went in his life. The Mother Superior of the Nunnery had employed a new groundsman and he and his family were anxious to take up residency in the quaint little house.

....

Nino's pistol skills had developed into fast competitive firing rounds with his father. He excelled so much so that he was able to seek out well-paid work as a marksman-artist in a travelling big top displaying all his skills taught to him by his father. The troop he travelled with felt like family; they cooked for each other, entertained each other and regaled each other with stories of their lives. Having travelled the Americas for over two years, Nino had been summoned home by telegraph to attend urgently for the sake of his father, who had uncharacteristically taken to his bed. Nino felt he had lived a good, honest life to date; fortunately, he had little overheads through his lifestyle of being on the road. Given full bed and board on the big top, he had some savings tucked away in a bank.

Working the big top wasn't always a walkover, though; he had to help with the installation and rigging, then the packing away, until his shoulders and arms grew quite muscular. The wonderful, curious crowd sat very quietly for him when he was under the spotlight. Nino tried to be as ethical as possible, only working with props and never animals, as he felt firearms and animals did not mix.

In his final year, he had introduced two lady twins into his act to demonstrate that his left hand was just as proficient as his right. They brought an element of glamour into his display and made staging more fun. They had stayed on while Nino had to return home.

Thankfully, in all his time away from home, he had never seen the inside of a jail; he had always kept on the right side of the law, helped by the fervent prayers of the nuns at the nunnery, he was sure.

He led his horse to a tethering rail, then loosened his pistol belt. His first point of call in this town was the sheriff's office, where he handed over his firearms to the deputy, declaring that he would be in town overnight as he was en-route to California and that he and his horse just needed to be fed and watered, to find a comfy bed for the night in the town boarding house. He tipped his hat to the deputy as he left the office and looked for a livery to put up his horse and keep some of his belongings from the old house.

He wore a matching black denim cowboy suit with silver detail, a black fedora cowboy hat with a red Mexican ribbon trim and his father's beloved red patterned sarape cloak to complete the array. The tavern was not full, so quiet that the portly barman was checking off stock on the bar, pencilling his crib sheet. He looked up reluctantly at the disturbance; Nino put him at ease with a broad smile.

"Yes, muchacho—what will it be?"

Nino politely requested, "Milk." The bartender put his pencil down and repeated the order. "Milk?" he said.

"Yes, please," Nino replied. The bartender turned around to go out back, his large grey and black Damask waistcoat shining as he disappeared into the kitchen area.

"Good day," called a little floozy with red ringlets and a flouncy dress on. Nino touched his hat. Soon she sidled up next to him. Nino rolled his eyes. "Go get some penny candy," he said, brushing her off quietly. The girl, who couldn't have been more than seventeen, he added, "I'm not going to stand on my head for you today, sister. Go get some stick candy." She obeyed and hurried through the swing doors. He turned back to the bar.

"Here is your drink, Señor." A young lady stood behind the bar with a tall glass of cool milk on a small tray. She kept her eyes downward. She wore a green bandana on her head, holding back a sea of thick long brown curls.

"Where is the bartender?" Nino enquired, as he had not finished his order.

"He is out back," she said, glancing up. Then, after a second of hesitation, she added, "I was curious to see the muchacho who ordered the milk." She smiled. Nino grinned openly; he knew he had sides to him and that he was never going to be a run-of-the-mill cowboy due to his past.

"I'm passing through," he said, laying his cards on the table.

"I don't see a gun..." she enquired.

"That's because I am a law-abiding citizen. What line of work do you think I'm in?"

"I thought— I thought maybe a bounty hunter. But there is no star," she said, looking puzzled.

"That's a fair guess. You *could* earn good money doing a job like that: $250 a month maybe. But I believe it would take up too much of my time and resources - If I were to keep them alive, I would have to bed down next to a criminal each night and I don't want to associate myself with such riff-raff and end up feeling dirty just like them, just for the purse. If they were dead, I would have to haul their rotting corpse for miles in sun baked terrain and my horse wouldn't take too kindly to that." The young lady smiled.

"I have no joy in seeing a man hang at the end of a rope either." Nino bent his rangy torso over the bar to take up the glass.

"I can help you with your order – what more would you like?"

"What's your name?" Nino enquired.

"Deardra," she replied.

"Deardra, can you serve up a good steak?" She nodded. "I will be back shortly," and she began to go.

"Oh," Nino added. She turned back. "What about a helping of peach cobbler, do you bake?"

"Yes, it is possible," she said, glancing back one last time before disappearing behind the string curtain divider.

Nino smiled; for the first time in a long time, he was at his ease. Somehow he knew he was at a crossroad in his life today. Now he wanted nothing more than a stable home life, a decently built homestead, the love of a good woman and a job that wouldn't put his life on the line at the toss of a coin.

He was to be a 'County Linesman' now that he had left the troop. This new up-and-coming trade gave him the freedom he craved: 'to work from the sweat of his brow' building up a fledgling network of telegraph poles bringing telecommunication to the masses. To be his own boss out in the terrain meant a lot to him but also, finally being able to put down some roots and go home each night to the love of a good woman meant a lot also. He wanted a well-kept home to put memories of his Marksman 'Big Top' days in an Ottoman of his own, to have a wife, good grub and children born on the right side of the sheets; it suddenly meant the world to him and didn't seem impossible to attain.

When Deardra returned, they both hunkered down—sitting at a small round table nearest the bar, she enquired, "The Sarape Cloak you're wearing?"

"It was my father's."

"It's handwoven—very beautiful." She noted.

"Apparently, my mother made it for him some time ago. He's just passed. I laid him to rest yesterday."

"I'm very sorry," she said, searching his eyes. Nino told her of his plans to head for California to take up the job offer to be a Linesman. "The one good bit of advice I was given is not only to learn how to read the terrain but to keep ahead of the weather. In the winter months, there are blizzards. When you feel the weather turn and that northern wind start coming on the plains in the circuit of Nebraska or Omaha, you don't want to get caught up in any chill wind or snow that's coming. You've got to jump on your horse and get out of there with your coat tails flapping," he said, smiling at Deardra.

He then enquired after her family, her hopes and ambitions. Then after helping him pick at the peach cobbler, she rose to clear the table. When she came back, she brought with her a photograph of her parents on their wedding day. "This is very special to me—my mother recently passed also," she sat down with Nino again. Nino took up her hands in his—

there was no need for more words around the subject of loss, as both their lives seemed to mirror each other. Their shared empathy put them on a level footing. "Is there anything else I can get you before you meet my father?" she asked.

"I must compliment you on the good spread."

"Thank you," she retorted, smiling broadly.

"Yes," Nino said, smiling back. "Why don't I push the boat out?" He leaned back in his chair. "I think I'd like a tankard of your draft sarsaparilla." It's time to bite the bullet, he thought to himself. Leaning in again, looking earnestly at Deardra. "Will you join me?" he enquired.

That's My Man

Bryce rose early that Monday morning; he ate his breakfast of warm grits left out for him by his parents, who had already left for work. Then he washed up to get ready for school. But firstly, this seven-year-old had a job to do. He grabbed a Tupperware container wrapped in a brown bag on the kitchen counter alongside his lunchbox. At the front door, he collected his shoe-shine toolbox and boarded a Chicago bus across town, past Navy Pier, where the skyscrapers clawed upward into the sky and by the subway, where scores of busy commuters disappeared into the underbelly of the sidewalk.

He liked Mondays in particular, as men tended to want to make a fresh start and have their shoes shined and looking tip-top for the start of the week. He opened his shoe-shine toolbox, pulled out his polishing cloth and waited patiently there on the stoop for a customer, wrapping the polishing cloth around his hand.

Bryce was a Negro boy of Louisiana heritage with olive skin and shortish, coily dark brown hair. He had heavily lashed doe eyes and an angular face similar to a regular cut diamond with a point at the chin. Even at this young age, one could see the determined young boy was an organised go-getter. After sitting at the stoop for two hours every weekday morning, he would have made plenty to hail a cab to get him to school in good time before the nine o'clock bell.

He paid no attention to the sling backs, pumps, or moccasins; there was only money to be made from leather shoes, the black and brown lace-up Oxfords with real leather soles, accompanied by a well-turned-out demob suit—these men were oftentimes the best tippers.

Today was a special day – as it was always on Mondays Mr Ellsworth, his well-to-do neighbour, would make a point of stopping by his stoop, away from the footfall crush of the sidewalk. He always carried a leather briefcase and a newspaper under his arm. Emerson Ellsworth was an American; he had dark brown Roman curls and surprising green eyes under a thick brow – he was clean-shaven and 'type A' thin. He was a man who could not sit around too long – the only thing that held his interest was a good game of baseball on the television or an energising session of lengths in his swimming pool. He prided himself on being the Press Office Manager for Rhadope Lifestyle magazine. In his world of work, others would refer to him as a semi-mogul as he had a clipped accent that no one would expect to switch into a southern lilt but this only ever happened when he was referring to food, as he spoke the way his negro wet nurse – Albertha – addressed him whilst organising meals for the hired help of the family when he was in her charge at his home as a child. "I have a hankering for some good soul food," he said, leaning in. "You know I could murder a plate of collard greens and ham hocks," he said with a broad smile, raising his left foot onto the wooden footrest. Bryce found it funny that such a well-to-do American businessman would even know about collard food so intimately. He gave a broad smile back, handing over the brown package, which contained a portion of his family's Sunday lunch.

"I will eat like a king today," Emerson pronounced, putting the package under the arm of his dark brown suit with striped detail and matching waistcoat. He had on a felt brown Homburg hat, which he tilted upwards while eyeing his vintage timepiece. He liked to stay ahead of the pack and prided himself on being the Press Office Manager, always being the first one in and the last one out. "Good job," he commended Bryce, patting his woolly curls. "See that you get along to school after 'stoop watch,' OK? Thank your mother, Luella, for saving me some of her delicious cooking."

"I will," Bryce said, folding up his dollar bill.

After his 'stoop session,' Bryce laid all the paper notes neatly together, folding them in half and placing them in the front of his left loafer. Mr Ellsworth was one customer who always gave him proper paper money, even though the shoe shine was worth only a quarter. Something he appreciated.

………

Bryce's parents worked next door to the Ellsworths as a double act, maid and butler team, so they were out of the home by 5 a.m. each weekday morning. Their quarters—a quaint single-story attachment at the rear of the sprawling family home belonging to the Zimmerman family, a doctor and a stay-at-home mother of two.

Because of the unique living situation Bryce's parents found themselves in, they were able to squirrel away over half of their monthly pay cheque towards Bryce's college fund.

Car wash day was an event; both Zimmerman cars would be lined up along the side of the house, a good spot to soap and hose down the family's Chevrolet and Cadillac. Bryce would make a point of trying to race his father, Ashcombe, into finishing first; someone would take pity on him, usually one of the taller Zimmerman boys and quickly soap the tops of the cars in a race for time. A sight his mother, Luella, found comical and charming. Bryce's uncle from Detroit, Michigan, would come to visit them from time to time, staying the whole day and giving himself the job of inspector and referee. Just when they were ready to call it quits, exhausted and wet, he would interject, "It ain't done unless the wheels are polished and shining too." When all had quieted down, Luella would reward the men by bringing out tall Tupperware cups of lemonade.

When the neighbours saw the amazing finish on the Zimmerman cars, they would come-a-calling for Bryce to do a number on their cars too, including the Ellsworths from next door with their green T-Bird. Bryce's little shirt and tank top would be wet through with perspiration but he slept well knowing his odd job money was accumulating nicely.

When Bryce was not cleaning up after the world, he would be found in his bedroom at his desk, doing his 'making'—painstakingly cutting out card using sharp little scissors, all of which his parents had facilitated. He cut and pasted airplanes and other 3D models of radios and anything around the house that took his interest, with great attention to detail; his models had to be seen to be believed. The Berwick family knew he was a boy ahead of his time, not entirely sure of where his gifting would lead him but they knew it would be dynamic.

Emerson and his wife, Elvira, had no children of their own for years prior to moving there but an accident involving close family friends Urwin and Almara West changed all of that. Their four-year-old daughter, Babbett, trapped in the car, was the only survivor of the horrendous scene. Due to the shock of the incident, the little girl lost her ability to speak and communicated using her eyes and hands to point out things. Emerson and Elvira had to display a colossal amount of patience, assuring themselves that after the legal adoption, she would slowly start to thrive and gain a feeling of well-being and regain the gift of speech.

Now an overnight father, Emerson went to great lengths to keep Babbett's identity and circumstance a secret—even moving to this out-of-the-way leafy gated community. There were no photographs of them as a family in the public arena and both parents made a point of sending her to regular school so that she could be with ordinary children like Bryce, the boy next door.

Now, having just turned seven, Babbett sat with her family in the den on a white floral-covered sofa. Emerson presented Babbett with the final boxed present. He placed it on the thick glass coffee table. "What is it?" he whispered by her ear. Babbett, in a white lacy chambray dress and white baby doll shoes, knelt on the thick rug before it. As she pulled at the pink satin ribbon and lifted the lid, she gave a gasp. In the white box, sat on top of cotton wool, was a light brown curly-haired cocker spaniel puppy, only three weeks old. "You can pet it." Elvira, her mother, encouraged.

Babbett reached inside the box with cupped hands and made an effort to lift out the adorable pup, which she placed on top of the box lid at eye level and it proceeded to sniff her button nose with his. This helpless animal could barely stand but relaxed when she took it up and rested it on her neck. "Are you happy with this, kitten?" Emmerson enquired. Babbett nodded her head briskly.

Later, the family sat in the den, Emerson reading a broadsheet with his pipe in hand and Elvira sat in an armchair knitting. A game of baseball was on the telly with the sound turned down. Babbett was sitting on the rug with a large square pouffe behind her with clawed feet. She raised the pup in the palm of her hand, kissing its large floppy ears, then set it down on the floor. The puppy lost its footing and flopped to the side. With a snicker, Babbett picked up the pup again and words came out of her mouth, "You're funny!" she exclaimed.

Immediately, Emerson looked over his newspaper at Elvira. Elvira raised her head from knitting with a look at him of recognition; there were tears in both their eyes and then the tears dried away to reveal broad smiles. The puppy had inspired Babbett to speak again. In the following months, as the puppy grew bounding about, Babbett was right there beside it. It was remarkable—the two became inseparable. She was allowed to bring the hound with her to school each day; the teachers saw for themselves the wonderful transformative effect the love of a pet could ignite in a young child.

………

"Everybody ought to know…" Luella sang out.
"Everybody ought to know," the quire sang back.
"Everybody ought to know…" she sang again.

"Who Jesus is," they sang in unison, "who Jesus is. He's the Lily of the valley, He's the bright and morning star..." they sang on.

The group wore textured white choir robes. Happy with the arrangement, they began strolling off the altar to make their way back home to their families. The majority had lye-permed hair set up in beehives or bouffant hairstyles with a large 'kiss' curl on their brown foreheads.

When Louella drove home into the rear of the Zimmerman house, she saw her husband Ascombe standing in front of his bird coop. She parked and went to join him with an open smile.

"How was your practice?" he enquired, acknowledging her return.

"I think we're there, all ready for Sunday," she replied, with her cream cardigan perched on her bony shoulders. Even in wedged heels, she still had to look up to see Ascombe's eyes. He held a turtle dove in his hand and blew gently at its face. "Hold out your hand," he instructed.

"Now Ascombe, you know I can take or leave these birds."

"Take this one," he said, putting it carefully on her little finger. He fed it a crumb straight away and the bird chirped happily.

Louella looked on at Ascombe with admiration; the birds brought out the best in her husband. "Now will you please do me the courtesy of taking this bird away so I can do my chores?" Ascombe snatched the bird off her with one smooth gesture and pecked his wife on the lips. "That pot of black-eyed peas you left on the stove should be ready now."

"It's had time to simmer nicely, I'm sure. Thanks for keeping an eye on it for me."

....

The Emmerson's had organised a sweet 16 birthday party for their daughter Babbett. The Zimmermans, Luella, Ascombe and Bryce attended. Luella took charge of the catering, bringing the traditional vol-au-vents, lobster rolls and buffalo wings; she also brought her Louisiana Creole cuisine, consisting of cornbread, shrimp rice, fried catfish and chicken and sausage gumbo.

Babbett enjoyed gifts of a pearl necklace and matching earrings, a bunny fur evening jacket and matching clutch purse and a white embroidered lace bedspread from the Berwicks.

With celebrations over, they could encourage their daughter to take driver's ed.

"Change into a land girl dress and wear your pumps," Elvera called. "You have eight minutes until your instructor arrives," Elvera said as she stood by the landing.

Babbett was excited to be entering this new chapter of her life; now she had something else to get excited about other than school Spelling B. She pulled her brown hair up into a ponytail.

"Don't forget to take your glasses - you'll need them," Elvera appeared at Babbett's bedroom door holding a pair of horn-rimmed glasses. "Mother, must I?"

"When you pass driver's ed, you can upgrade to contacts. Your father and I are keen to get them for you as a birthday present."

"OK, Mother," Babbett said, rolling her eyes.

"This is something very different for you to try your hand at. Promise me you'll be careful?"

"Yes, Mother, I will." They shared a quick embrace, then Babbett bounded down the stairs for her lesson. Her mother descended slowly after her with a look of pride.

·········

"I invited you up here, Bryce because I would like to talk with you man to man," Emerson said in the 'Rhadope Lifestyle Magazine' office. "Take a seat." He invited the young Bryce to sit opposite him. Bryce pulled off his newsboy cap; today he donned a cream and green horizontal block stripe knit polo sweater that clung to his muscular frame with heavy fishtail trousers. He slung his ankle over his left knee and grabbed it with both hands, revealing his cream penny loafers.

"Thank you, sir." He looked directly at Emerson.

"I have known you nearly all your life and it's important to me that you and your family are ok. I hear your grandfather's been taken ill - he's having to slow down somewhat. Your father tells me he needs your bedroom to accommodate him. Fortunately, you are all there in a single-story attachment, which will make life a little easier for him."

"That's the situation, sir."

"Well, I happen to have a very good solution for your problem and it will help all involved. Did you know that above here," Emerson said, pointing upwards with his right finger, "we have some apartments?"

"No, sir, I did not."

"Yes, there are six penthouse suites all along the top floor of this building and we own one of them."

"I see," Bryce said, nodding.

"I have always admired your entrepreneurial mindset – even as a child, you always astounded me with your work ethic, your drive and ambition…what makes it so compelling is that I have been right at your side and I don't remember one instance in which you were not prepared to roll up your sleeves and buckle down to the task at hand. You're a hard worker – and I respect you greatly for that."

"Thank you, sir."

"Well, I don't want to beat about the bush any longer; I just want to know if you're happy to come and work for Rhadope Magazine this summer now that you have graduated. I will put you on our staff rota straight away - with all the benefits, access to the gym, a maid to deal with all your laundry and 24/7 front door watchman assistance. What do you say?"

Bryce was smiling from ear to ear.

"I guess that's a 'yes,' Emerson said, smiling. "Welcome on board."

And so it was, after Bryce had passed his driver's ed and completed his degree major at OCU, Emerson invited Bryce to join him in the bustling press office as one of three graphic designers.

Emerson's daughter Babbett also graduated with a PA and Secretarial Skills major and joined the company to work alongside Cara, who had been in the PA role for many years. She was ironing out a job share with Human Resources over six months, giving time for Babbett to get comfortable in the role.

Now Babbett was on hand to escort her father out of the office when the office clock buzzed 5 PM on the dot.

Working with her father and her next-door neighbour Bryce seemed like a home away from home; they were always on hand for one another, which helped to abate any work stress and made for an even more relaxed atmosphere, with lots of praise and encouragement for the youngsters from Emerson.

·········

Dorett was the daughter of the Senior Sales Associate who had helped win the contract for this new printing firm— Denison Print & Distribution. They had managed to beat other contenders by issuing a competitive quote because they were out of state, based in Illinois, where printing overheads were much less. Their outfit also ran late into the night, while many others finished at 6 PM, ensuring a large print run and just-in-time delivery.

Due to ill health, Dorett's father had coached his daughter in print small talk and sent her along in his place in person with the contract letter stating their terms. This was usually done by post but Dorett's father liked the personal touch when sealing a deal.

·········

Bryce had just turned the latch key at his apartment that morning when the elevator bell chimed from afar. He had just finished locking the apartment door when he saw, to his utter surprise, a young collard woman in an orange Chanel coat making her way down the hall to him.

"I'm sorry." She gasped. "I seem to be lost. I am expected at Rhadope Magazine at nine but I have lost my way," she said, clasping the white envelope containing the Printer's Terms and Conditions in her gloved hand.

Bryce explained that she must have come in the wrong entrance.

"And you live, you live up here?" she enquired, taken aback.

"Let's just get you to where you need to be," he said, beckoning her with his hand back towards the elevator area. "Go back down to the ground floor lobby this time, take the left and another left to the front of the building's main sidewalk. Go through that business entrance and 'Rhadope' Magazine is all along the 8th floor."

Dorett was a little disappointed at having to go out of the building as it had started raining when she had entered. Once in the lift, she pulled out a silk scarf from her handbag and gently covered her beehive and cream disc earrings.

Babbett was sitting at the reception, reading through an array of newspapers looking for a mention of their Lifestyle Magazine in order to organise clippings for the Press Office Album. "Good morning, can I help you?" she enquired of the lady who came out of the lift.

Dorett's wet kitten heel shoe sank into the sumptuous office carpet as she stepped forward out of the lift. To the reception desk, she asked the girl there for Mr Ellsworth. "He's expecting my father but he fell ill. I'm the daughter of Mr Bowford, Senior Sales Associate for Denison Print & Distribution."

"Please follow me; I'll show you to Mr Ellsworth's office."

"Good morning," Emerson said, not sure if he had double booked the 9 a.m. slot.

"I'm here on behalf of my father, Mr Bowford," the young lady said briefly, clasping Emerson's hand in a firm shake. "Oh, I see…any trouble getting here?"

"The train." She gasped. "It was a tortuous journey, I can't lie - in the rush hour too. It was somewhat of a challenge." She smiled; her red lipstick complemented her brown skin.

"Please take a seat…now what's this business with your father being under the weather?" Emerson asked when she had settled.

"It's a burst appendix."

"My word! How long do you think he'll be out of the game?" he asked, looking at the large white envelope.

"Any queries you have can be addressed by him straight away. My father requested a telephone in his hospital room – he's awaiting your call right now," Dorett said, handing him the package.

"Well, that's good to know," Emerson said, standing and crossing the room. "I hope he regains his health soon. Thank you for bringing this all the way – I'll see you out," he said, holding the office door open.

"My pleasure." As Dorett exited the room, her eyes caught sight of Bryce at the far corner of the office. "All the best," she said and smiled at Emerson, then waited until he had closed his office door behind him before scurrying past desks over to Bryce's corner of the office. "I'm here all alone," she blurted. "I haven't got a friend in this city. Would you like to accompany me to the refectory?" she asked Bryce. "You do have a canteen here?" Bryce was taken aback. "Oh," he exclaimed, resting his arm at an angle on his draughtsman desk where he had been working on his artwork; he carefully placed down an ascertain sheet neatly, keeping his eyes fixed on the task in hand. He replied slowly, "You know, I think I'll pass—I have so much to organise here…deadlines, you know."

Dorett processed the information. "I know," she said, backing up, raising her purse defensively. "Sorry to have troubled you." She turned about on her heel and disappeared back across the press office floor.

Bryce was not happy with this exchange but at the penthouse, he had noticed her painted stocking line up the back of her legs. His mother had pointed out to him, "A girl with a back seam to catch the eye is categorised 'wild' and in need of a lot of the wrong sort of attention." This woman would not go down well with Mother or the church folk. Besides, he was settled in this job and could not consider for a minute doing anything so ridiculous to arouse suspicion and lose the trust of his manager, Mr Ellsworth, who was like a father to him.

Lunchtime was special to him. He rested on the draughtsman chair. He liked to amble along to Babbett's reception desk and wait sheepishly while she came off the phone or finished her task. They would go to the canteen together; he liked holding the canteen door open for her. She was always conservatively dressed for work. No bodycon dresses for her but regular lumberjack-checked day dresses and sensible peep-toe bow pumps. He even liked that she wore horn-rimmed glasses to drive. He had known her for so many years growing up; he knew she was 'a safe pair of hands.' His mother and father knew her story and simply adored her too.

That evening, Bryce made his way home. He liked to take in the air and walk around the outside of the building to the apartment's front entrance rather than use the internal maze of corridors and service lifts. As he entered his apartment, he noticed that it turned and opened with only one turn of his latch key - he was sure he had locked it that morning. Nonetheless, he proceeded into the fashionable interior. When he threw a housewarming party, his father slapped him on the back. They laughed with his mother, who ran from room to room with outstretched gloved hands declaring, "Oh Sweet Jesus," "There is a God," and "Praise be." Her eyes were on stalks that day; he had never seen her so proud.

"I'm in here, darling," he heard a voice call out from the bedroom. In disbelief, he ran to the bedroom and staggered back in the doorway in shock.

"I thought I would stick around this town a little longer. I want to get to know you better…I realise you were busy today at the office. Now don't be a killjoy, come in and join me – I know you want to." It was Dorett holding up the cream satin sheet around her torso, laid out on the bed.

"NO – I don't want to join you," Bryce shot back. "Kindly pull on your clothes and scram, get out of here."

"We were the only blacks in that office today! Does that not mean anything to you? Why do you treat me like a stranger?"

"Look," Bryce retorted, "I don't know you from Adam. How did you get in here?"

"You foolishly left a spare key under the large plant by the door."

"That was not me. That was someone else who stayed here before."

"Well you know who cares," she said, getting agitated talking to the empty doorway. "Won't you join me?"

"I hardly know you."

"I'm Dorett…" she said, rolling her eyes. "I tried to get acquainted this morning," she said, reaching for a sip of water. "Look, I'll show you all you need to do - don't be shy."

"You're too fast for me," Bryce said clutching at the nape of his tie.

"A virgin," she shot back, laughing. "I knew it," she said, spilling water on the sheet. "There is no little black book, no condoms in these bedside drawers, no naughty magazines under the bed," she rolled on. "No panties under the sofa cushions…"

"Please get dressed," he said, staggering backward into the hall. Perspiration began to sting his face. He felt shame - he covered his eyes with one hand.

Had he not done the right thing all his life? He was not about to change, not even if this disgusting rendezvous was laid out on a platter for him, as it was.

"Leave my apartment," he said, raising his voice. "I'm not bluffing…I swear I'll call the cops."

With that, Dorett shot a look of disdain at the empty doorway and proceeded to pull on her underwear. "What a square." She mocked, pulling on her pencil skirt. "OK, I'm leaving," she shouted, pulling on her shoes and collecting her coat from a clear resin chair beside the wardrobe. She brushed past Bryce and stormed to the door. When he saw her turn left toward the lobby escalator, he ran behind her.

"Are you crazy – not that escalator, the back stairwell," he said, pointing with his thumb.

"Right down to the first floor. Follow the internal corridor to the office lobby, they are there until seven. G o n o w."

………

"Why the long face, Kitten?" Emerson asked Babbett when he arrived home from work; he found her curled up on the armchair.

"Who was the collard lady today at the office?" she enquired.

"Oh, she was the daughter of a Sales Rep. He couldn't make it in himself; he sent her in with the Terms of Agreement paperwork and Invoice."

"So she won't be coming back again to the office?"

"No, I think not. Is that agreeable to you?" he asked, taking off his cashmere coat.

"Father, I don't want any trouble – but for the first time, I'm feeling a little possessive towards Bryce." Her eyes glazed over. "I think I want him to be more than just a friend. I don't want any trouble," she blurted. There was a wet tissue in her hand.

"But you want your man," he said, taking off his hat; he was smiling. "Bryce is a good kid; if I'm honest, you could do no better – you two have got history, that's for sure," he said, giving her a reassuring pat.

"I like him too," he said. "He's like the son I never had."

"Oh, Father." Babbett sighed, leaving the armchair and giving him a hug. "I'm so glad you understand."

As Emerson put away his coat in the hallway, the telephone rang. "I'll get it from the hall," he called to Babbett in the den.

"You gotta help me, Sir."

"Slow down, is that you, Bryce?"

"You gotta help me, Sir," he repeated. "I just turned up at my apartment and there she was – in my bed – buck naked."

"What?" he exclaimed. "Who?"

"I gave her no encouragement; I only spoke to her a couple of times today at the office. I turned her down when she asked me to take her to the refectory."

"You mean Dorett Bowford," he said, aghast. Babbett ran out into the hall. "What's the matter, Father?" Emerson quickly cradled the mouthpiece of the telephone. "Take yourself upstairs to your room and don't come out until I call you." Babbett and the hound ran up the stairs with urgency. Babbett knew something terrible had happened; she had never seen that look on her father's face before. She tried with all her will to obey her father but she lingered in the corner of the landing, waiting to hear if Bryce was okay.

"Put that chain on your door. I'm glad you didn't carouse with her. We need to come up with a plan to get this situation resolved, mid to long term. Give me an hour; I will call you back. I need to put a call in to an old friend."

Bryce ran out to the escalator and made his way down to the lobby reception. He patted away the perspiration that had collected over his brow and tried to regain composure.

"That woman you sent up to my apartment," he said to the night watchman.

The guard immediately raised his hands, owning up. "She said she was Kin – have I done something wrong?"

"She is a stranger – she's a predator. You sent her up and she found a key to my apartment under a plant; she let herself in for heaven's sake. I could have your job for this." The guard's eyes bulged. Bryce took a breath and softened. "But you know what I'm gonna do? I will give you a chance. But you must promise me never to breathe a word about this to anyone. Please don't let anyone up to my apartment again if I am out. Got that?"

"Yes, sir."

"Under no circumstances."

"Got it," the Guard said.

·········

"I've never seen such a scrap," Chrispen said to his wife as they sat watching the baseball. "Extraordinary," he said, pulling out a cigar from the breast pocket of his robe. His wife took a sip from her large brandy glass; they had just settled to watch the second half after a commercial when the phone rang. He went over to the sideboard and picked up the receiver. He stood and listened to Emerson, an old college buddy, as he spoke directly down the telephone to him. "This needs to be handled with the greatest care. One must remain dignified – as if playing a supreme game of chess. Yes. This is a seminal moment."

·········

Emerson and Elvira talked on the landing outside Babbett's door. "It's the only way these kids will have a prayer." They entered the room; Elvira joined Babbett on the lacy cover of the single bed, whilst Emerson remained standing. "Babbett, do you trust your mother and me?" he asked her directly.

"Yes, Father, you know I do."

"Then you must do as I say - to the letter." He began to explain to her what had transpired during that day. "This is a monumental decision," he said. "Show no emotion now, no sentimentality. You are fighting for your life, your future happiness that was promised to you by the Universe as a child – it must come to fruition."

....

"You must eat something, dear," Elvira said to Babbett.

"No, Mother, I'm ready now. Please, let's get this over with."

"Here's my Cocktail Swing dress," she said, laying out a white dress in a clear see-through zipped bag. "The one I wore on the cruise last year. Oh, I do hope it fits. I could try to pin in the bodice for you; try it on for me now…"

....

And so there was a wedding held in the dead of night amongst a small company: Luella, Ascombe and their church reverend. Elvira and Emerson also stood in their best attire to mark this pivotal occasion. "And before God and this company…I now pronounce you Bryce and Babbett – man and wife."

"Congratulations," the parents shook hands. "God bless you."

The pair caught the Pan Am red-eye to Anchorage, in Alaska. "Damned man-eater," Babbett said as she sighed a sigh of relief. "I finally have an excuse to buy fur," she said in a lighter tone, folding her arm into Bryce's. They both sat with their heads nestled together. "When we settle into the company condo, I would like to present you with a husky," he declared. They both laughed. "We can do all of that and more," Babbett said.

....

Chrispen had created two openings in his company's press office for a secular lifestyle magazine. All involved were happy to give the kids a chance; they had been safely ensconced in pastures new.

....

Lastly, I will share with you a personal account of my parents' life in late 1960s England, Hackney – Fremont Street E9. I invite you all in with a true account of a heroic feat involving my father, Malcolm Thomas Hicks, from South America – Guyana. Making him my hero.

....

Thank you to Hackney Archives, Library and Heritage Services. Dalston CLR James Library, Dalston Square, London E8 3BQ.

**Photograph
Of my father and Jamie**

My Hero

"Run a bath for me…" Malcolm said on entering his house with the key still in the door. He looked frazzled; his black woolly hair was matted and his clothes were soaking wet under a rough grey speckled blanket given to him by a hospital attendant. Faye, who had been pacing the floor by the door for some time, worried by the lateness of her husband's arrival, piped, "I thought you were visiting your mother – why are you so late – what has happened to you?" she asked, closing the door.

"I was on my way, just as I told you – to do my errand and then to make the 'B' line to my mother's – but on the way, there was an incident. I never got to her house at all." He was uncomfortable in the clothes that clung tightly to his limbs but offered a reassuring clasp of both his wife's shoulders as he stumbled in his wet shoes, squelching.

Faye turned on her heels and ran up to the bathroom, doing what had been instructed. "You're not hurt?"

"No, not me – I helped a young child today," he said, peeling off the wet garments. Faye reached for her head tie at the back of the bathroom door; she covered her bouffant hair just before the room was engulfed in hot steam. She poured some bubbles into the water and the bath rapidly filled. Malcolm wasted no time stepping into the hot, welcoming bathtub as he immersed his tired limbs. Faye ran out to get him a stiff drink from the downstairs drinks cabinet. When she got back, he looked more like himself and had begun relaxing. "I was walking along Hackney Road on my way to visit my mother when I witnessed a young boy being bullied by some lads bigger than he. I saw them throw the boy's new bike into the canal." Malcolm gulped the drink down from the shot glass while Faye sat on the clothes basket, eyes wide with concern.

"Then all I see is the boy jumping into the water going after the bike. The other boys cleared off and left him for dead. The boy fell into difficulty as the water was deeper than he expected." Malcolm paused to wash his face. "I was standing on the bridge above. I quickly signalled for the oncoming traffic to halt as I attempted to make a running jump over the bridge."

"Dear Lord," Faye exclaimed, holding her face in her hands.

"I dove into the river and swam out to the boy. I got to him just before I lost sight of his head and pulled him out. If you see the traffic, there were people everywhere, just looking. We had to get an ambulance and it took us to the hospital. We both had to have a tetanus jab there and then, before they let me go."

"And the boy – is he OK?"

"Jamie was shaken up, in shock, sad to lose his bike but he'll live," Malcolm said, soaping his body frantically. "Hear this: a reporter from the Hackney Gazette wants to run the story – can you believe it?" They both chuckled, Faye leaning sideways on the top of the basket. "So you're famous now?" she jibed, laughing. "Wait till your mother hears this," she pronounced, slapping a thigh.

Much later that evening, after listening to his favourite Ace Cannon record, the melodic tones of the American saxophonist had soothed away the stress of the day. Malcolm turned his attention to a Jimmy Cliff record now, in a jubilant mood.

"That little boy's life was nearly snuffed out…" he declared, "but we are both here to tell the tale…Better Days are Coming," he sang out, grabbing Faye in an embrace.